This book belongs to:

_____

_____

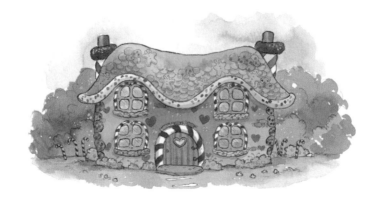

A Collection of
Favourite
Tales

A Collection of
Favourite
Tales

A Treasury of Favourite Stories

Produced for Chad Valley Toys
242-246 Marylebone Road
London, NW1 6JL

www.woolworths.co.uk

ISBN 1-40545-996-4

Printed in China.

Illustrated by Bill Bolton, Diane Catchpole, Daniel Howarth,
Jan Nesbitt, Gillian Roberts and Rory Tyger

Stories retold by Gaby Goldsack and Alison Boyle

Contents

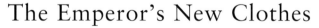

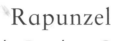

The Ugly Duckling

It was a beautiful summer's day. The sun shone brightly on Mother Duck as she lay her eggs. "Quack, quack," she went, as she stood up to count the eggs. "Gosh, that egg is a really big one," she thought. "It will probably turn out to be a big strong drake, like Father Duck." Happy, she settled back down on her nest.

Mother Duck had been sitting on her eggs for a long time when, suddenly,

CR . . . ACK

CR . . . ACK, the eggs began to hatch. One by one, the yellow ducklings appeared. Soon, Mother Duck had four beautiful fluffy babies. Now only the really big egg was left.

Mother Duck sat patiently on the really big egg until, at last, CR . . . ACK, out burst a duckling. But my, what an ugly duckling it was! It was large and grey, and not at all beautiful like the others. "Hmmm," thought Mother Duck, "perhaps it isn't a duckling after all. I'll take it to the water and see."

"Follow me," called Mother Duck. One, two, three, four, five . . . the ducklings hurried after her. SPLASH! She jumped into the river. "Quack, quack!" she called out, and all the ducklings splashed into the water. Soon all of them, even the ugly grey one, were swimming along.

Next, Mother Duck introduced her babies to the other ducks around the farmyard. "Now, my dears," she said quietly, "bow your heads and say 'quack' to the Old Duck."

All the ducklings, even the ugly grey one, did as they were told. But the other ducks just laughed when they saw the ugly duckling.

"I've never seen anything so ugly," said one.

"What is that?" asked another.

"Come here," called the Old Duck to Mother Duck. "Let me see your children. Hmm! All are very pretty, except that big one."

"He might be ugly," said Mother Duck, "but he swims well."

"Such a pity!" sighed the Old Duck.

Life around the farmyard was very happy for the four yellow ducklings. But the ugly duckling had a terrible time. He was very unhappy. All the ducks and hens teased him because he was so ugly, and no one ever let him join in the fun.

One day, the ugly duckling decided to run away. He scrambled down to the river and began to swim as fast as he could – away from the farmyard, away from Mother Duck and away from the four beautiful yellow ducklings. Soon he met two wild geese. "You are ugly," laughed the geese. "You are really so ugly that we cannot help but like you. Won't you come and fly with us?"

But the ugly ducking couldn't leave with them because he didn't know how to fly.

Cluck, cluck!

Hiss, hiss!

He walked on and on, until he came to a hut. Inside the hut lived an old woman, a cat and a hen.

"Hiss, hiss!" went the cat.

"Cluck, cluck!" went the hen.

"What, what?" went the old woman. "Look's like we'll be eating duck's eggs from now on."

And so the ugly duckling was allowed to stay. Of course, no eggs appeared. The hen and the cat teased the duckling.

"Can you lay eggs, like me?" asked the hen.

"No," replied the duckling.

"Can you purr, like me?" asked the cat.

"No," replied the duckling.

"Quite ugly! Quite useless!" went the cat and the hen together.

The ugly duckling wandered back to the river where he spent his days alone. Soon, winter came and the weather became icy. The duckling grew tired and cold. One day a farmer rescued the ugly duckling and carried him home. The farmer's children tried to play with him but, thinking they were teasing him, he jumped into the milk pail. Milk spilled everywhere

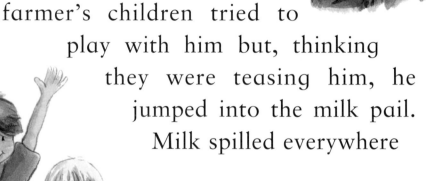

"AHHH!"

"Ahhhh!" screamed the farmer's wife.

"Ha! Ha!" laughed the farmer's children.

Luckily the door was open, and the duckling flew out.

The ugly duckling was happy when spring arrived at last. He flapped his wings and soared into the sky. Below, he saw a garden with a large lake in the middle. On the lake were some beautiful white swans.

"I must go down to them," thought the ugly duckling.

He landed on the water and swam towards the swans. They raced forwards to meet him. The duckling bent his head, expecting to be attacked. Instead, he saw

his own reflection in
the water. He could
hardly believe his eyes.
He was no longer an ugly
grey duckling. He was a beautiful white swan.

As the other swans fussed around their new friend, some children came to the water's edge. "Look, there's a new swan on the lake," cried one. "It's the most beautiful swan I've ever seen." Then the old swans bowed before the young swan. He had never been so happy in his whole life!

The Princess and
the Pea

Once upon a time, in a faraway place, there lived a handsome prince. Now this prince wanted to get married. But he didn't want to marry an ordinary girl. He wanted to marry a real princess.

The prince travelled from place to place in search of a wife. But the prince didn't know how to tell the difference between a real princess and a pretend one. He found lots of princesses but there was always something wrong with them. Some were too tall. Some were too small. Some were too silly. Some were too serious. There was even one that was too pretty!

After the prince had travelled far and wide, he began to think he would never ever find a real princess, and so he returned home. The prince became more and more unhappy. His father and mother, the king and queen, were very worried. They did not know what to do about their sad son.

Then one dark, stormy night there was a knock at the palace door. The old king himself went to open the door. You can imagine how surprised he was to find a soaking-wet girl shivering before him.

"Come in, come in," said the kind king. "Who are you? Why are you outdoors on such a terrible night?"

"Hello, I'm a princess," the girl told the surprised king. "I'm afraid I became quite lost in the storm. Please can I sleep here for the night?"

The king stared at the girl in disbelief. But the prince began to smile when he heard her musical voice and saw her beautiful smile. The queen looked carefully at the girl's dripping-wet clothes and wild straggly hair.

"Ah, we shall soon see whether you're a real princess or not," she thought. "There's one sure way of finding out." However, the queen did not tell anyone about her plan.

Quietly, the queen tiptoed into the guest bedroom. She took all the sheets and blankets off the bed and put three tiny peas on top of the mattress. Then she placed twenty more mattresses, one on top of the other,

over the peas. Finally, she put twenty feather quilts on top of the mattresses. The bed was so high that the poor princess needed a ladder to climb onto it.

The next morning, the queen asked the princess how she had slept.

"I hardly slept a wink last night," replied the princess.

"I had a terrible night. There was something very hard in my bed. I'm bruised all over."

Now it was obvious to the queen that only a real princess could feel three tiny peas through twenty mattresses and twenty feather quilts. Everyone agreed that she was indeed a real princess.

The prince was so happy to find a real princess at last, especially such a pretty one. They were married straight away and lived a long and happy life together. And as for the three peas – they were put into the royal museum, where you can still see them today. That is, unless they have been stolen by someone who wants to find a real princess!

The Gingerbread Man

Once upon a time there lived a little old man and a little old woman. The little old man and the little old woman were very happy except for one thing – they had no children. So, one day they decided to make a child for themselves. They rolled his body out of gingerbread, and used raisins for his eyes and nose, and orange peel for his mouth. Then they put him in the oven to bake.

When the Gingerbread Man was cooked, the little old woman opened the door and . . .

. . . out jumped the Gingerbread Man and away he ran.

"Come back! Come back!" cried the little old man and the little old woman, running after him as fast as they could. But the Gingerbread Man just laughed, and shouted,

"Run, run, as fast as you can.
You can't catch me,
I'm the Gingerbread Man!"

The little old man and the little old woman could not catch him, and soon they gave up. The Gingerbread Man ran on and on, until he met a cow.

"Moo," said the cow. "Stop! I would like to eat you."

"Ha!" said the Gingerbread Man. "I have run away

from a little old man and a little old woman, and now I will run away from you."

The cow began to chase the Gingerbread Man across the field, but the Gingerbread Man simply ran faster, and sang,

"Run, run, as fast as you can. You can't catch me, I'm the Gingerbread Man!"

The cow could not catch him. The Gingerbread Man ran on, until he met a horse.

"Neigh," said the horse. "Stop! I would like to eat you."

"Ha!" said the Gingerbread Man. "I have run away from a little old man, a little old woman and a cow, and now I will run away from you."

Then the horse began to chase the Gingerbread Man, but the Gingerbread Man ran faster and faster, and as he ran he sang,

"Run, run, as fast as you can. You can't catch me, I'm the Gingerbread Man!"

The horse could not catch him, so the Gingerbread Man ran on, until he came to a playground full of children.

"Hey, Gingerbread Man," called the children. "Stop! We would like to eat you."

"Ha!" said the Gingerbread Man. "I have run away from a little old man, a little old woman, a cow and a horse, and now I will run away from you."

The children began to chase the Gingerbread Man but it was no good, the Gingerbread Man was just too quick for them.

While he ran he sang,

"Run, run, as fast as you can.
You can't catch me,
I'm the Gingerbread Man!"

By now, the Gingerbread Man was feeling very pleased with himself. "No one will ever eat me," he thought, as he came to a river. "I am the cleverest person alive."

Just then, a fox appeared and came towards the Gingerbread Man.

"I have run away from a little old man, a little old woman, a cow, a horse and a playground full of children, and now I will run away from you," shouted the Gingerbread Man.

"Run, run, as fast as you can. You can't catch me, I'm the Gingerbread Man!"

"I don't want to eat you," laughed the fox. "I just want to help you cross the river. Why don't you jump onto my tail and I'll carry you across?"

"Okay," said the Gingerbread Man, and up he hopped. When the fox had swum a little way he turned to the Gingerbread Man and said, "My tail is getting tired. Won't you jump onto my back?"

So the Gingerbread Man did.

A little farther on, the fox said to the Gingerbread Man, "You are going to get wet on my back. Won't you jump onto my shoulder?"

So the Gingerbread Man did.

Then just a bit farther on, the fox said to the

Gingerbread Man, "Quickly, my shoulders are sinking. Jump onto my nose. That way you will keep dry."

So the Gingerbread Man did, and before he knew it the fox had flipped the Gingerbread Man up into the air and gulped him down in a single bite.

The poor Gingerbread Man wasn't so clever after all, was he?

The Golden Goose

Once upon a time, there was a woodcutter who lived with his wife and their three sons. The two oldest sons were clever, and spoilt by their parents. But the youngest, who was called Dan, wasn't so clever or spoilt. Indeed, his mother, father and brothers laughed at him.

One day the woodcutter was unable to work in the forest, so he sent the eldest son in his place. His mother, who loved her eldest son dearly, packed him a fine lunch of sausage rolls and lemonade and waved goodbye to him.

Before starting work, the eldest son, who was a lazy boy, thought it would be a good idea to have a little bite to eat. So he sat down on a log and laid out the fine food his mother had packed for him. But before he had time to take a bite, an odd little man popped out of nowhere.

"Share your food with a hungry beggar?" asked the man, licking his lips and rubbing his hands together.

"Go away!" snapped the eldest son, who was mean as well as lazy. "This is my food, and I'm not sharing it with anyone, especially a funny little thing like you."

"Well really," said the little man. "Nothing good will come from being so greedy and mean." And, do you know, that's just what the eldest son found out for himself when, after finishing all the sausage rolls and swigging all the lemonade, he cut himself badly and had to go straight home without any wood.

35

The next day, the middle son was sent to cut wood in his brother's place. Once again, his mother packed a fine lunch for him. Once again, as he sat down to eat, the funny little man popped out of nowhere and asked for a nibble. And, because the middle son was no kinder than his brother, the little man was again told to go away.

Which was a mistake because the middle son also cut himself badly and had to go straight home without any wood. For you see, the little man was a magician.

On the third day, the woodcutter had no choice but to send his youngest son, Dan, to cut wood in the forest. This time, the mother couldn't be bothered to pack a fine lunch, for she considered that anything nice was wasted on her youngest and (in her opinion) silliest son. So she gave him nothing more than a crust of stale bread and a bottle of sour milk and told him he was lucky to get anything at all.

This time, when the little man popped up to ask for a bite to eat, Dan said, "I am afraid it is a very simple meal but you are more than welcome to share it with me. I always like making new friends."

So, you can imagine his surprise when he unwrapped the food to discover that the tiny scrap of stale bread and the bottle of sour milk had magically turned into yummy sausage rolls and lemonade. Dan and the little man ate and drank until they could eat and drink no more.

"You've been fine company, and I always say that one good turn deserves another," said the little man. "So why don't you cut down that old tree over there? I do believe you will find something interesting beneath it."

Dan chopped down the tree, and do you know what he found beneath it? A goose with feathers of gold!

"Wow!" Dan exclaimed, and turned to thank the little man. But he had vanished.

Dan knew that if he took the golden goose home his brothers would take it away from him. So instead of going home, he decided to walk the world in search of his fortune.

After his first day's travelling, Dan found an inn where he could stay for the night. The innkeeper and his three daughters would have stolen the golden goose from Dan – but he never let it out of his sight, not for a single minute.

The next morning, Dan plucked a golden feather from the goose and paid for his lodgings with it. Then he tucked the goose under his arm and left. As the landlord's eldest daughter watched him walk down the road, she thought, "Hmm! Just one of those feathers of gold would buy me a very fine dress indeed." So she raced after Dan and reached out to pluck a feather from the goose's tail. But, do you

know, as soon as she touched the goose, she couldn't let go.

"Let me go! Let me go!" screamed the girl.

But Dan just strode on, saying, "I can't stop now, I've got a whole world to explore."

So the girl screamed and shouted, until her sisters came out to see what the commotion was about. They grabbed hold of their eldest sister and tried to pull her away. But as soon as they touched her, they, too, were stuck fast.

Dan strode on, ignoring the girls' cries. Then, as they were passing through the village, the parson saw what he thought were three girls chasing a boy. "Disgraceful behaviour!" he cried, and caught hold of the girls to pull them away. But, as I am sure you have guessed, as soon as he touched the last girl in the line, he was stuck fast.

And so it went on and on, until Dan and his goose had quite a following. There were the landlord's three daughters, the parson, a schoolteacher, a village blacksmith, a bellringer, four shopkeepers, thirteen housewives... Together they marched on and on

until they reached the city where the king lived.

Dan had heard that the king had a daughter who, though very beautiful, was always sad and never laughed. This made the king so unhappy that he had promised her hand in marriage to whoever made her laugh.

Dan was used to making people laugh without even trying, so he was sure that he could bring a smile to the princess's face.

Boldly, he marched right up to the palace, and into the courtyard. You should have seen how people pointed and laughed to see Dan and his golden goose being followed by such a long line of struggling people.

They laughed so much that the princess came to see what all the fuss was about. When she saw Dan and his goose, with the long tail of stumbling, struggling people following close behind him, her lips began to twitch and before she knew it, she was roaring with laughter. In fact, it wasn't a very ladylike laugh at all. But the king didn't mind a bit, and he said that Dan and the princess should be married at once.

Dan never forgot the odd little man, and when he eventually became king, he never forgot that "one good turn deserves another."

The Emperor's New Clothes

A long time ago, there lived an emperor who loved clothes. He loved them so much that he spent all his money on them. He had a different suit for every hour of the day. He cared about nothing else.

One day, two dishonest men came to the emperor's kingdom. They said that they could weave the finest cloth in the whole world. The cloth would be so fine that it would be invisible to anyone who was either stupid or not good enough to do their job.

The rumours about these men soon reached the ears of the emperor.

"I must have some of that cloth," he thought. "Not only will it make me look splendid, but it will also help me find out which of my men are stupid or not good enough for their job."

So the two rogues were invited to the emperor's palace. They set up their looms and were soon hard at work pretending to weave the cloth. They asked for the very finest silks and the purest gold and silver thread. Of course, these materials all went straight into the rogues' bags. This was all one big joke – there is no such thing as invisible cloth.

The emperor was keen to see how the weavers were

getting on, but he was also afraid. What if he saw nothing? Would that mean he was stupid? Would that mean he was unfit to be emperor? Before visiting them, he decided to send his first minister. He was such a clever man that he was sure to see the cloth.

When the first minister entered the room where the two men were weaving, he looked and looked but could see nothing. "Gracious," he thought. "Does this mean I'm stupid? Does this mean I'm unfit to do my job? No one must know. I will pretend that I've seen the cloth."

Then he listened very carefully as the rogues described all the fine patterns and colours in the cloth. Later, the first minister repeated their words to the emperor.

When he heard how magnificent the cloth was, the emperor decided to see for himself. He took all his ministers, including the first minister, and entered the weaving room.

The emperor looked and looked but, to his dismay, he could see nothing. "Oh, my!" he thought. "Does this mean I'm stupid, or does it mean I'm unfit to be emperor? Either way, nobody must ever know." And so, he too decided to pretend that he could see the invisible cloth.

"Wonderful! Marvellous!" he cried out loud. As the first minister pointed out this colour and that design, the other ministers looked and looked but, of course, they could see nothing. None of

them dared admit to being stupid or unfit for their job, so they also praised the cloth. "It's beautiful," said one. "You really should have some clothes made from it for your annual procession," advised another.

The emperor soon agreed and the two weavers set to work and pretended to make a fine suit for the emperor. They worked long into the night on the days before the procession. They waved scissors here and needles there. Everyone was very impressed because the two rogues worked so hard.

Finally, the day of the procession arrived. The whole city was talking about the emperor's new suit. People couldn't wait to see it for themselves. More importantly, they couldn't wait to see which of their friends and neighbours could see it, and which of them could not, proving they were either stupid or unfit for their job. The whole city was buzzing.

The suit itself was ready just in time.

"The cloth is as light as a feather. It's so light that you could almost imagine you were wearing nothing," explained one of the rogues. Then he helped the emperor into first the trousers, then the jacket.

"I'm sure you'll agree that the suit is magnificent," said the other rogue, making the emperor, who was really quite naked, twirl around in front of the mirror.

The emperor turned this way and that, trying to see if he could catch the merest glimpse of the suit. But it was no good, he could still see nothing. Aloud he said, "It's splendid. Quite the finest suit I own."

"Yes, splendid," agreed his first minister. "You've never looked more royal."

The emperor did not want anyone to know that he was unfit to do his job. Convinced that he was, indeed, dressed in a most splendid suit, the emperor held his head up high and went to join his procession.

As he marched through the street, all the people watching cried out, "Just look at the emperor's new clothes. They are the most beautiful we have ever seen." No one would admit that they could not see the clothes. They were afraid that if they did, everyone would know they were either stupid or unfit for their job.

Then, at last, a child pushed to the front of the crowd and began to point at the emperor and laugh.

"But the emperor's got nothing on," he giggled.

A ripple went through the crowd. Suddenly, everyone knew that the child was right. There was the proud emperor walking naked through the streets of the city. Everyone began to point at him and laugh.

Even the emperor knew that they were right. But he did nothing for fear of looking even more stupid. He just carried on walking and pretended he was wearing his favourite suit. Wasn't he a silly emperor?

49

The Frog Prince

Once upon a time, there lived a young princess. She had lots and lots of toys but her favourite one was a golden ball. She carried it with her wherever she went.

One day the princess set off for a walk in the woods. When she grew tired, she sat down beside a pool to rest. As she sat there, she threw her golden ball into the air and caught it. Higher and higher she threw the ball, until one time it soared so high that she couldn't catch it. SPLASH! The ball fell into the pool. The princess peered into the dark water but it was so deep that she couldn't see the bottom.

"Oh, no!" wailed the princess. "My ball is lost. I

would give anything – even my fine clothes and jewels – just anything to have my ball back."

Just then she heard a noise,

"RIBBET! RIBBET!"

A frog popped its ugly head out of the water and spoke, "Dear Princess, what is wrong? Why are you crying?"

"Eeeek!" screamed the princess. She was not used to meeting frogs that could talk. "Wh . . . what can a nasty frog do to help me? My golden ball has fallen into the pool. Now it is gone for ever!"

"Don't cry," croaked the frog. "If you will just let me eat from your plate and sleep on your pillow, I will find your ball."

"Hmm!" thought the princess. "This slimy frog will never be able to get out of the water. If it finds my ball, I won't have to do any of those silly things." So she turned to the frog and lied, "If you bring back my ball, I promise to do everything you ask."

At that, the frog ducked beneath the water. In no time at all, he was back with the ball in his mouth. He threw it at the princess's feet. Delighted, the princess snatched up the ball and ran home as fast as she could. Not once did she think to say thank you to the frog. Indeed, she forgot all about him.

"Wait for me!" croaked the frog. But the princess was gone.

The next evening, as the princess sat down to dinner, she heard a strange noise:

PLISH, PLASH, PLISH!

It sounded as if something wet was coming up the stairs. Then there was a TAP, TAP on the door and a little voice croaked,

"Open the door, my one true love.
Open the door, my turtle dove.
Remember the promise you made in the wood
Well now is the time to make it come good."

The princess opened the door and there stood the frog. Feeling frightened, she slammed the door in his face.

"What's the matter?" asked her father, the king.

The princess told him all about her lost ball and her promise to the frog.

"You must always keep a promise, my dear," the king said to his daughter. "Go and let him in." So the princess opened the door.

The frog hopped in and ‿PLISH, PLASH, PLISH!‿ made his way to the table.

"Lift me up to sit beside you," said the frog. Wrinkling her nose, the princess did as he asked.

"Push your plate closer so that I can eat from it," said the frog. Closing her eyes, the princess did as he asked. When the frog had eaten as much as he could, he croaked, "I'm tired. Carry me upstairs and let me sleep in your bed." With a large frown on her face, the princess did as he asked.

Within minutes, the frog was snoring away on the princess's pillow.

And there he slept until it was morning. Then he

zzZZZ zZZZ

awoke and hopped away without so much as a R I B B E T. "Hooray!" cried the princess. "That should be the last I see of that jumped-up tadpole."

But the princess was wrong. That evening, the frog knocked on the door once more, and croaked,

"Open the door, my one true love.

Open the door, my turtle dove.

Remember the promise you made in the wood.

Well now is the time to make it come good."

The princess opened the door and in hopped the frog.

PLISH, PLASH, PLISH!

Once again, he ate from the princess's plate and slept on her pillow until morning.

By the third evening, the princess was beginning to like the frog a little. "His eyes are quite lovely," she thought, as she drifted off to sleep.

But when the princess awoke the next morning, she was astonished to find a handsome prince standing beside her bed. The frog was nowhere to be seen. As she gazed into the prince's strangely familiar eyes, he explained how an evil fairy had cast a spell on him and turned him into an ugly frog. The spell could only be broken when a princess let him eat from her plate and sleep in her bed for three nights.

"Now you have broken the spell, and I wish to ask for your hand in marriage," said the prince.

Being a princess, she quickly agreed, and before the prince could say "RIBBET", a fine coach and a handsome horse appeared. Together they rode off to the prince's home where they lived happily ever after.

The Little Mermaid

Long ago, deep below the ocean blue, there lay the kingdom of the mer-people. The mer-people were similar to humans, but instead of legs they had tails like fish. At the centre of the kingdom stood the mer-king's splendid palace. Inside the palace lived the mer-king, his mother and his six mermaid daughters. The six princesses were all beautiful, but the youngest was the fairest of them all. She was also blessed with the sweetest of voices.

The little mermaid loved to hear about the human world. She would spend many hours listening to her grandmother's stories about sailors and their huge ships, about busy towns and animals that walked on the land.

"When you are fifteen," said her grandmother, "you will be allowed to go to the surface of the sea, and see all these things for yourself."

Year after year, the little mermaid looked on as her sisters reached their fifteenth birthday. One by one, each mermaid made her first journey to the water's surface.

At last, the little mermaid's fifteenth birthday arrived. As she rose to the water's surface, she saw a large ship at anchor. Its decks were alive with men dancing and singing noisily. Among the men was a handsome prince. It was his sixteenth birthday and the whole ship was celebrating.

The little mermaid watched the handsome prince late into the night. Then the ocean began to bubble and swirl. A storm arrived, and the big ship was tossed from wave to wave.

Suddenly, the ship was thrown onto its side and began to sink. The little mermaid realized that the men were in danger, but it was so dark that she could not see what was happening. As the ship plunged below the waves, the little mermaid spotted the unconscious body of the prince. Ignoring the danger, she swam to his side and caught hold of him.

The mermaid swam and swam until she reached the nearest shore. She dragged the prince onto a sandy beach and then slipped back into the sea and waited.

Early the next morning, a group of young girls came out of a large white building by the beach to walk along the water's edge. Before long, one of the younger girls found the prince. She knelt beside him as he began to wake up. How the little mermaid's heart ached as the prince smiled up at the young girl. He thought it was she, and not the little mermaid, who had saved him. The little mermaid felt so sad that she plunged beneath the waves and returned home.

Day by day, the little mermaid became more and more unhappy. At last, she revealed her secret to one of her sisters. Soon all the other mermaids knew her story.

Luckily, one of them knew where the prince lived, and was happy to show the little mermaid the way to his palace by the sea.

After the little mermaid had found her prince's palace, she used to return there most evenings. Hidden by darkness, she would watch him from the water as he stood on his balcony overlooking the sea. The prince grew more and more dear to the little mermaid. However, she knew that he could never love her, for to be admired by a human she needed two legs instead of a tail.

One day, the little mermaid decided she would risk everything to win the prince's love. So she went to visit an evil witch.

"I know what you want," cackled the witch. "I will prepare you a drink that will give you legs instead of a tail. However, whenever you walk it will feel as if you are walking on broken glass.

Do you agree to this?"

"Yes!" cried the princess.

"If the prince marries another, your heart will break and you will turn into foam on the sea," added the witch. "It will be as if you never existed. Also, you must pay me with your voice."

"But how will I charm the prince without my voice?" asked the little mermaid.

"What do I care?" cried the witch. So the little mermaid gave away her voice in return for the witch's potion. Unable to speak or sing, she headed to the prince's palace. Once there, she drank the witch's potion. She felt it run through her body like sharp knives, and then she fell down in a swoon.

When the little mermaid awoke, her tail had been replaced with legs. She stood up to walk and found that the witch had been right – every step felt as if she was walking on broken glass. However, when she came across the prince, she forgot her pain. The prince asked the little mermaid who she was but, of course, she could not speak.

The prince was delighted with the little mermaid, and took her with him everywhere he went. However, he looked upon her as a sweet child and never thought of making her his wife. He would tell her how he wished to marry a young girl who had saved his life after a shipwreck. "I saw her only once," he would say, "but she is the only one I can ever love. She is the girl I wish to marry." The little mermaid was unable to tell him that she was the one who had saved his life.

One day, the prince's parents arranged for him to sail to a neighbouring kingdom to marry a princess. "Don't worry," he told the mermaid. "I must go but it is impossible for me to love her. If I cannot have the girl I love, I will marry you."

However, when the prince saw the princess, he cried out, "It is her! She is the one who saved my life." It was decided that they should marry without delay.

The little mermaid was very sad. As she watched the prince and his bride marry, she wept silent tears. Later, after everyone else was asleep, her sisters appeared. They had lost their beautiful golden hair, and their heads were shaved bare.

"We have made a deal with the witch," said the eldest sister. "We have given her our hair in return for this knife. If you plunge it into the prince's heart, you will become a mermaid again."

The little mermaid loved the prince so dearly that she could never think of taking his life. Throwing the knife aside, she leapt into the ocean. However, instead of dissolving into foam, she found herself floating gently upwards. Around her were many beautiful wispy shapes. Then she saw that she too was like them. The little mermaid had been so sweet and good that she had earned herself a place in heaven.

The Wind in the Willows

The Mole had been spring cleaning his underground home all morning. His fine coat was splattered with whitewash, and his arms were tired. From outside his underground home, he could hear the spring calling to him. Suddenly, he threw down his brush and cried, "Hang spring cleaning."

He charged out of the house and scrabbled through the tunnel that led to the outside world. At last, POP, the Mole came out into the sunshine.

"This is better than whitewashing," he said to himself, as he ran across a meadow. The Mole ambled along until he came to a river. He'd never seen a river before. He was fascinated by the way the water gurgled and gleamed. Mole sat on the grass and gazed at the bank opposite, until a dark hole caught his eye.

"What a fine home that would make!" he thought. As he continued looking at the hole, something twinkled, then winked at him. It was an eye. An eye that belonged to a little brown face. It was the Water Rat.

"Hello, Mole," called the Water Rat.

"Hello, Rat," called the Mole.

"Would you like to come over?" asked the Rat.

"How?" replied the Mole.

The Rat said nothing, but pulled out a tiny boat and stepped into it.

He was soon at the Mole's side. The Rat held out his paw and helped the excited Mole into the boat.

"I've never been in a boat before," said the Mole.

"What?" cried the Rat. "Well, what have you been doing then?"

"Is it really that nice?" asked Mole.

"It's the only thing to do," said the Water Rat. "Believe me, my young friend, there is nothing – absolutely nothing – half so much worth doing as simply messing about in boats. I know. Why don't we go down the river together?"

The Mole was overjoyed. "Let's go at once!" he cried.

So the Rat fetched a large picnic basket and they were off.

"What's in the basket?" asked the Mole.

"There's cold chicken," began the Rat, "coldtonguecoldhamcoldbeefcoldpickledgherkins saladFrenchrolls . . ."

"Stop, stop," laughed the Mole. "It's all too much."

The Rat rowed downstream, while the Mole took in all the new sights and sounds. "What's over there?" he asked, waving a paw at a wood in the distance.

"Oh, that's the Wild Wood. We river-bankers don't go there if we can help it."

"Why not?" asked the Mole nervously.

"Well, some of the rabbits in there aren't bad. And Badger lives right in the heart of it. Dear old Badger. Nobody would mess with him."

"Who would want to mess with him?" asked the Mole.

"You know, the usual – weasels, stoats and foxes. You can't really trust them."

"And what's beyond the Wild Wood?" asked the Mole. "The Wide World," said the Rat. "But I'll never go there, and neither will you if you've got any sense. Ah, here's our picnic spot."

The Rat tied the boat up to the bank and helped the Mole ashore. Soon they were both tucking hungrily into their picnic. Before they had finished, the Mole had met two of the Rat's good friends. First, there was the Otter who declared the Mole a friend of his own before departing. Then there was the Badger, who grunted "Huh, company," before making a hasty retreat.

Toad was also out on the river. He was testing out a brand-new rowing boat – and not making a very good job of it. "It's another of his fads," explained the Rat.

"Whatever it is he soon gets tired of it, and starts on something new."

Soon it was time to leave. As the Rat rowed gently home, the Mole grew more and more restless.

"Ratty! Please can I row now?"

"Wait until you've had a few lessons," smiled the Rat.

The Mole was quiet for a minute, then he leapt up and snatched the oars from the Rat.

"You'll have us over," cried the Rat. And as the Mole swung wildly about with the oars, SPLASH, that's just what happened.

The Mole sank, came spluttering to the surface, then sank once more. Then a strong paw reached out and hauled him onto dry land. It was the Rat. Laughing, he dried the Mole off then plunged back into the water to save the boat and the picnic basket.

When the Mole took his seat in the boat once more, he felt quite ashamed and apologized to his new friend.

"Don't worry about it," said the Rat cheerfully. "You know, I think you should come and stay with me for a while. I'll teach you how to row and swim. You'll soon get used to it. We'll have a wonderful time."

The Mole was so happy that he burst into tears. The Rat pretended not to notice.

When they got home, the Rat lit a cosy fire and told the Mole river stories until suppertime. After a fine supper, a tired and happy Mole went straight to bed.

The following days were similar to Mole's first day on the river. He soon learned to swim and row. Each day, he had fun messing about on the river. Each night, as he drifted off to sleep, he was comforted by the sounds of the river lapping at his windowsill and of the wind whispering in the willows.

Hansel and Gretel

There was once a poor woodcutter, who lived in the forest with his wife and two children, called Hansel and Gretel. The woodcutter loved Hansel and Gretel dearly, but his wife felt quite differently about them. She was their stepmother, and wished they had never been born.

One cold winter, there was not enough food in the woodcutter's house, and everyone was hungry. One night, after the children had gone to bed, the stepmother said to her husband, "Something has to be done, or we will all starve.

Tomorrow you must take the children into the wood and leave them there."

"No," gasped the woodcutter. "I couldn't do such an evil thing to them."

But the wicked stepmother wouldn't leave the woodcutter alone until he had agreed. Luckily for Hansel and Gretel, they heard their stepmother's wicked plan.

"What shall we do?" sobbed Gretel.

"Don't worry," said Hansel, who had been looking out of the window. "I have an idea." He slipped out into the garden, put a handful of white pebbles into his pocket and then crept back to bed.

The following morning, Hansel and Gretel followed the woodcutter and his wife deep into the forest. Along the way Hansel kept stopping to drop a pebble onto the ground.

73

When they reached the middle of the forest, the woodcutter made a fire and told the children he would return at the end of the day. Of course, he never did.

Night fell, and strange sounds filled the forest.

"How shall we find our way home?" sobbed Gretel.

"Don't worry," said Hansel. "Wait until the Moon rises."

When, at last, the Moon began to shine, the white pebbles twinkled like stars. As Hansel had planned, they followed the pebbles all the way home. The woodcutter was overjoyed at his children's safe return.

Shortly after, the family had even less food in the house. Again, the children heard their stepmother say to their father, "Tomorrow you must take the children farther into the wood and leave them."

After much argument, their father agreed. When they had gone to sleep, Hansel tried to go outside to collect some pebbles, but his stepmother had locked the door.

The following morning, the children were each given a crust of bread and told to follow their father into the forest. As he walked, Hansel dropped breadcrumbs behind him.

Eventually, their father led them to a different part of the forest. "I'll be back when I've finished work," said the woodcutter. Of course, he never returned.

"Don't worry," Hansel said to Gretel. "When the Moon rises, we will be able to follow the breadcrumbs home."

However, when the Moon rose there were no breadcrumbs. The birds of the forest had eaten them. Hansel and Gretel wandered in the forest all night long, but they got more and more lost. Eventually, they grew so tired that they lay down to sleep.

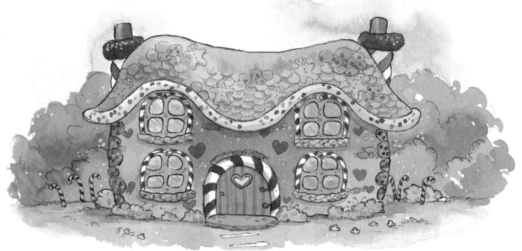

In the morning, the children walked deeper into the forest until they came to a little cottage. It was made of bread, cakes and sweets! Hansel and Gretel were so hungry that they began to break bits off to eat. Suddenly, the door swung open and out burst a witch.

"Gotcha, you nasty nippers," she cackled, grabbing Hansel and Gretel. "You think you can scoff my house, do you? We'll just see how you like being eaten." Then she dragged the children into her cottage and threw Hansel into a cage. "When he's big and fat, I'm going to eat him. Ha, ha, ha, ha!"

Over the next weeks, the witch gave the very finest food to Hansel, but she gave Gretel only scraps and bones. Gretel gave one of these bones to her brother. "Hold it when the witch asks for a finger to feel how fat you are," said Gretel. "She is so blind that she won't know the difference." Gretel was right, and the witch was amazed that Hansel did not grow fatter. Then, one day, she could wait no longer.

"Fat or thin, I'm going to eat him," she cackled. "Light the oven, Gretel."

Weeping, poor Gretel did as she was told. Soon the fire beneath the oven was blazing.

"Is it hot enough yet?" asked the witch, who was beginning to grow hungry.

"I don't know," said Gretel. "How can you tell?"

"Out of my way, you stupid girl," growled the witch. She pushed Gretel aside and stuck her head in the oven. Quick as a flash, Gretel pushed the evil witch into the oven and slammed the door shut.

Gretel quickly found the witch's keys and released Hansel. Then they used the keys to open all the chests in the witch's cottage. Inside they found gold, silver and precious stones.

"Father should be able to buy

all the food we need with this," said Hansel, filling his pockets.

Once more, the children set off in search of home. They walked through the forest for a long time. Then, at last, they came to a place they knew and were able to find their father's cottage. Their father, whose wife had left him, was overjoyed to see them. His happiness was even greater when he saw the treasures that Hansel and Gretel had brought.

"Aaah! We need never go hungry again," he cried, hugging Hansel and Gretel. And from that day, they knew nothing but happiness.

79

Rapunzel

Along time ago, a man and his wife were expecting their first baby. As time passed, the wife spent much of her day resting. She would stare out of the window into a beautiful garden filled with wonderful flowers and herbs. No one ever dared to enter this garden because it was owned by a horrible witch.

One day, as the wife was looking into the garden, she noticed a clump of a delicious-looking herb. It was called rapunzel, and it looked so fresh

80

and sweet that she could almost taste it.

In the days that followed, the woman spent more and more of her time gazing at the rapunzel. Before long, she grew quite miserable.

"What's wrong, my dear?" asked her husband.

"I want to eat the rapunzel in the witch's garden," she replied. "I think I'll be ill if I don't have some soon."

The man couldn't bear to see his wife suffer, so that night he tiptoed into the witch's garden, grabbed a bunch of rapunzel and ran back home.

His wife was overjoyed. The rapunzel tasted so delicious that she wanted more. So the next night, her husband once again tiptoed into the witch's garden. He was just about to pick the rapunzel when an ugly-looking figure jumped out at him – it was the wicked witch.

"Caught you, you thieving toad," she cackled. "You'll regret ever sneaking in here and stealing my rapunzel."

"Forgive me!" cried the man. "My wife is expecting a baby. She told me she would fall ill if she couldn't eat some of your delicious rapunzel."

"A baby, eh?" grinned the toothless witch. "Hmm! You may take as much rapunzel as you like, but you must give me your baby once it is born. If you don't agree, I will turn you and your wife into toads."

The man had no other choice, and so he quickly agreed.

Shortly after, the woman gave birth to a beautiful baby girl. The parents were overjoyed, but their happiness was short lived. As soon as they wondered what to

name her, the wicked witch appeared.

"She shall be called Rapunzel," cackled the witch. "And this will be the last time you'll ever see her." Then, with a final cackle, she took the baby and disappeared.

Rapunzel grew into a very pretty girl, with beautiful, long, golden hair. When she was sixteen years old the witch locked her in a room at the top of a very tall tower. The tower had no door or stairs. The only way in was through a single window.

Every day the witch came and stood at the bottom of the tower, and called, "Rapunzel, Rapunzel, let down your fair hair."

Rapunzel would then lower her long hair through the window, and the witch would use it as a ladder.

One day, a handsome prince was riding in the woods when he heard Rapunzel singing. The prince followed the beautiful sound until he came to the tower. But, finding there was no way in, he went away. However, he was so enchanted with Rapunzel's voice that he returned to listen to her day after day.

One day, as the prince was hiding in the trees, he saw the witch arrive and call out, "Rapunzel, Rapunzel, let down your fair hair."

Then he watched in amazement as Rapunzel's golden hair tumbled to the ground and the witch climbed up into the tower. The prince waited until the witch had gone and then he went to the tower.

"Rapunzel, Rapunzel, let down your fair hair," he cried.

At once Rapunzel's hair fell to the ground and up climbed the prince. Rapunzel was afraid when she saw the prince, but his kind words soon calmed her. "I heard your beautiful voice," he explained. "Now that I've seen you, I will not rest until you agree to marry me."

Rapunzel was quite in love with the handsome prince and quickly agreed. "First, I must escape though. Bring me some silk and I will weave a ladder. Then I will be able to climb down."

So each day, after the witch had left, the prince came

with silk. The witch suspected nothing until one day Rapunzel said to the witch, "You are so much heavier than the prince." As soon as she had said these words, Rapunzel knew she was in trouble.

"You wicked girl," screeched the witch. She grabbed a pair of scissors and cut off Rapunzel's long hair. Then she cast a spell whisking Rapunzel away to a far-off place.

That night, when the prince came to the tower, the witch was ready.

"Rapunzel, Rapunzel, let down your fair hair," called the prince. Holding on tight, the witch let Rapunzel's hair fall to the ground and up climbed the prince.

"Ahhh!" screamed the prince when the witch poked out her ugly head.

"Ha!" cried the witch. "Rapunzel's gone and you'll never set eyes on her

again." Then she let go of Rapunzel's lovely locks and the prince fell to the ground. Unluckily, some rose thorns pricked his eyes and blinded him.

In the years that followed, the blind prince looked everywhere for his lost love. One day, he heard the same sweet voice he had heard before. As he wandered towards it, Rapunzel saw her handsome prince again. She ran to him weeping. The prince gathered her into his arms and her tears fell into his eyes. At once he could see again.

The prince took Rapunzel back to his kingdom, where they married and lived happily ever after.

Tom Thumb

Late one night, a poor farmer and his wife sat talking in their kitchen. "It is a shame we have no children," said the farmer.

"Oh yes, dear," agreed his wife. "I'd be happy if we had just one child. I'd love that child even if it was no bigger than my thumb."

Not long after that, the wife's wish was granted. She gave birth to a baby boy. He was strong and healthy, but he was no bigger than her thumb. The couple were delighted and called their new baby Tom Thumb.

The years passed, but tiny Tom stayed the same size as the day he was born. Although he was very small, Tom was clever and helpful.

One day, the farmer was getting ready to go into the forest to cut wood. "If only I had someone to bring the cart along later," he sighed.

"I'll bring it," said Tom Thumb.

"But Tom," laughed his father. "You're far too small!"

"Don't worry," said Tom Thumb. "Just get Mother to harness the horse and I'll do the rest."

Later, after his mother had harnessed the horse, Tom asked her to place him inside the horse's ear. From there, Tom told the horse where to go. All went well, and soon Tom and the cart had reached the wood. Then, as Tom was shouting "Steady! Steady!", two strangers walked past.

"That's funny!" said one. "I can hear someone directing that cart. Yet nobody is there. Let's see where it goes."

89

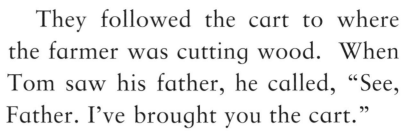

They followed the cart to where the farmer was cutting wood. When Tom saw his father, he called, "See, Father. I've brought you the cart."

The two strangers looked on in astonishment as Tom's father pulled Tom out of the horse's ear. "That little chap could make us our fortune," whispered one of the strangers. "We could take him from town to town and people would pay us to see him."

So the two strangers went up to the farmer and asked, "How much do you want for the little man?"

"I wouldn't sell him for all the gold in the world," replied the farmer.

However, on hearing the strangers' words, Tom had an idea. He climbed onto his father's shoulder and whispered into his ear, "Take their money. I'll soon come back." So the farmer gave Tom to the two strangers, and received a large bag of gold coins in return.

After saying goodbye to his father, Tom was carried off by the strangers.

They walked for a while until Tom said, "Put me down!" When the man did as Tom asked, the tiny boy ran off and hid in a mouse-hole.

"Goodbye!" shouted Tom. "You should have kept a closer eye on me."

The two men searched for Tom but it was no good. At last, they gave up and went home without him. Tom crept out of the mouse-hole and walked along the path until he found a barn, where he went to sleep in the hay.

The next morning, the milkmaid got up to feed the cows. She went to the barn and grabbed an armful of hay – the same hay in which Tom was sleeping. Poor Tom knew nothing about it, until he found himself inside the stomach of one of the cows.

It was a dark place. And more and more hay kept coming into the cow's

stomach. The space left for Tom grew smaller and smaller. At last, Tom cried, "No more hay!"

The milkmaid ran to the dairy farmer in fright. "Sir, the cow is talking," she cried.

"Are you mad?" asked the farmer, but he went to the barn to see for himself.

"No more hay!" shouted Tom. This bewildered the farmer, who sent for the vet.

The vet operated on the cow and out popped a bunch of hay. Tom was hidden inside it. The hay was thrown onto the manure heap. Just as Tom was preparing to escape, a hungry wolf ran by and gulped down Tom and the hay.

Refusing to give up hope, Tom spoke to the wolf, "I know where you can get a mighty feast."

"Where?" asked the wolf.

Quickly, Tom described the way to his father's house.

That night, the wolf climbed in through the farmer's

kitchen window. Once inside, he ate so much food and grew so fat that he couldn't squeeze back out of the window. This was just what Tom had planned. He began to jump around in the wolf's stomach and shout as loud as he could.

Very soon, the farmer and his wife were awoken by the noise. They rushed into the kitchen. Seeing the wolf, the farmer grabbed his axe and aimed at the wolf. Suddenly he heard Tom's voice, "Father, I am inside the wolf's stomach."

Overjoyed, the farmer killed the wolf with a single blow to his head. Then he cut

Tom out of its stomach.

From that day onwards, Tom stayed at home with his parents. Now he knew for sure that there is no place like home!

Little Red Riding Hood

Once upon a time, there was a little girl who lived with her mother in a tiny cottage on the edge of a large wood. The little girl's grandmother had made her a beautiful red cloak with a hood, so people called her Little Red Riding Hood.

One day, Little Red Riding Hood's mother asked her to take a basket of food to her grandmother, who wasn't very well. She lived on the other side of the wood. It was a lovely day, and Little Red Riding Hood always enjoyed visiting Granny, so she waved happily to her mother and skipped away.

Little Red Riding Hood hadn't skipped very far when she stopped to pick some flowers for her

grandmother. Just then a crafty-looking wolf wandered by. "Hellooo, my lovely!" he smiled. "Where are you going on this fine day?"

"I'm going to see Granny who lives in the cottage on the other side of the wood," explained Little Red Riding Hood, who had not been told never to speak to strangers. "She's not very well, so I'm taking her this basket of food and a bunch of flowers."

"What a thoughtful girl," purred the wolf, trying to hide his sly grin. "Well, I must dash. See you!"

"Seems like a nice wolf, although he does appear to be in a bit of a rush," thought Little Red Riding Hood as she watched him race away. But then she forgot all about the wolf and skipped on through the woods.

Meanwhile, the wolf, who wasn't nice at all, ran all the way to Little Red Riding Hood's grandmother's house. "Oh, goody," he smiled, as he peeked through the window and saw Granny lying in bed. "It's almost too easy." He licked his lips and rubbed his rumbling tummy.

"Yoo-hoo!" he called, as he knocked on the door.

"Is that you, Little Red Riding Hood?" croaked

Granny, who had a sore throat. "Come in, the door's open. I've been expecting you."

With that, the wicked wolf pushed his way into the cottage and gobbled up Granny in a single gulp. Then, quick as a flash, he put on her spare nightdress and nightcap, popped on her glasses, and jumped into her bed.

A few minutes later, when Little Red Riding Hood knocked on the door, the wolf pulled the blankets up to his chin. "Come in, my dear," he called, in his very best grandmother voice. "The door is open."

Little Red Riding Hood skipped into the house. "I've brought you some yummy food, and…" Little Red Riding Hood stopped in her tracks when she caught sight of her grandmother.

"Oh dear, Granny, what big eyes you've got," she said, feeling just the tiniest bit afraid.

"All the better to see you with, my dear," replied the sneaky wolf.

"But Granny, what big ears you've got," she whispered, beginning to feel very afraid.

"All the better to hear you with, my dear," replied the wolf, trying not to snigger.

"And Granny, what big teeth you've got," she squeaked, now feeling absolutely terrified.

"All the better to EAT you with," roared the wolf, as he leapt from the bed.

Little Red Riding Hood managed one ear-piercing scream before the wolf pounced and gobbled her up in a single gulp.

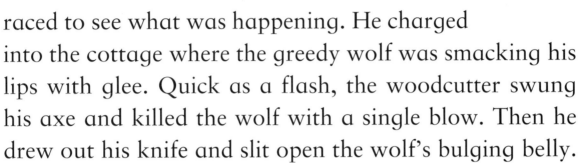

Out in the forest, a passing woodcutter heard the loud scream and raced to see what was happening. He charged into the cottage where the greedy wolf was smacking his lips with glee. Quick as a flash, the woodcutter swung his axe and killed the wolf with a single blow. Then he drew out his knife and slit open the wolf's bulging belly.

Out popped Little Red Riding Hood and her grandmother. Granny was so pleased that she invited the woodcutter to tea.

From that day on, Little Red Riding Hood never talked to strangers again – especially ones with big eyes, big ears, and big teeth!

Cinderella

Long ago, in a distant land, there lived a man with his beautiful daughter. They were both very happy, until one day the man took a new wife. The new wife was not a kind woman and, to make matters worse, she had two bad-tempered daughters.

The two daughters were so mean and so ugly that they were jealous of the man's beautiful daughter. Indeed, they were so jealous that they took away all her fine clothes and forced her to work as their maid.

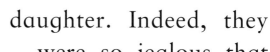

The poor girl worked from

dawn to dusk. She cooked all the meals, cleaned all the rooms, and looked after all the fires. And when she wasn't working around the house, the ugly sisters insisted that she dress them and brush their hair.

At night, while the ugly sisters snored in their fine beds, their beautiful stepsister huddled among the cinders beside the fire. This was why she always looked so dusty and sooty and everyone called her Cinderella.

Now, one day the king's messenger brought an invitation to the house. It was an invitation to a ball that the king was giving for his son, the prince. All the young girls in the land were invited, so that the prince could choose a bride.

The ugly sisters were delighted, and immediately started discussing what they were going to wear.

"Can I come, too?" asked Cinderella. "I've never been to a ball."

"Of course you can't, silly," laughed Cinderella's stepmother, pointing to the rags she wore. "What would you wear? Besides, no prince would bother looking at a silly, sooty face like yours. But don't worry, you can help my girls get dressed for the ball."

On the evening of the ball, the ugly sisters took ages getting ready. Poor Cinderella's head whirled as they barked orders at her.

"Tighter, tighter!" cried one, as Cinderella struggled to fasten a corset around her huge waist.

"Ouch! That hurt!" snapped the other, as Cinderella tried to tease the knots from her tangled hair.

When at last they left for the ball, Cinderella fell to the floor and wept. "If only I could go to the ball," she sobbed.

"But you shall," said a kind voice. Cinderella wiped the tears from her eyes and looked up to see her fairy godmother standing before her.

As you can imagine, Cinderella was very surprised. She hadn't even known that she had a fairy godmother until that moment. "But I haven't got a thing to wear," she said. "And I haven't got

a coach, so I'd never get there in time."

"Just fetch these things," said the fairy godmother, pulling out a list from up her sleeve, "and I'll get you there before you know it."

Cinderella looked at the list and frowned. But, being a good girl, she quickly did as she was asked. Five minutes later, she returned with the things on the list: a pumpkin, six white mice, a frog and two lizards.

Her fairy godmother drew out her magic wand and touched the pumpkin. Immediately it turned into a golden coach.

Then she touched the mice with her wand, and they turned into six white horses. Next she touched the frog, which turned into a smart coachman. And finally, she touched the two lizards, who turned into two well-dressed footmen.

"And now for you," said the fairy godmother, pointing her wand at Cinderella. Instantly, Cinderella's rags were transformed into a fine velvet ball gown, and the clogs she usually wore on her feet were turned into delicate glass slippers.

"Now, go to your ball and enjoy yourself," said the fairy godmother. "But remember this. You must leave the ball before midnight, for on the stroke of twelve the magic will run out and all will be as it was before."

The footmen helped Cinderella into the coach, the coachman took up the reins, and they were on their way.

When Cinderella arrived at the ball, everyone gasped at her beauty.

107

"May I have this dance?" asked the prince. And, of course, Cinderella agreed. For the rest of the evening, the prince would dance with no other. Cinderella's ugly sisters didn't recognise her, dressed as she was in such fine clothes. But they were still furious. "I can't imagine what the prince sees in her. She's nothing but a skinny beanpole," sneered one.

"Barely a jewel in sight," sneered the other. It was the best evening of Cinderella's life. She enjoyed herself so much that she almost forgot about her fairy godmother's warning. Then, just before twelve, she remembered.

"I must leave," she told the prince.

Before he could stop her, she had fled into the night. But as she raced out of the palace, she slipped on the steps and lost one of her glass slippers. She dared not stop.

She didn't even notice that the prince picked up the slipper. Then, as the clock struck twelve, Cinderella's ball gown vanished and she found herself in her rags once more. When she got to where she had left the coach, she found the pumpkin in its place.

Poor Cinderella had to run all the way home. She only just made it before her stepmother and stepsisters returned.

The next day, the prince announced that he would travel the kingdom in search of the owner of the dainty slipper. "Every girl in the kingdom will try it for size," he declared, "for whoever it fits is the one I love, and the one I will make my bride."

Of course, every girl in the kingdom was eager to marry the prince. Girls of all shapes and sizes tried to squeeze their foot into the tiny slipper but it was too small.

At last, the prince arrived at Cinderella's house. Cinderella's stepmother was determined that one of her daughters would become the prince's bride.

"Push harder," she hissed, trying to wedge the glass slipper on one of her daughters' feet.

"Can't you do anything right?" she complained, when her other daughter couldn't even get the slipper over her knobbly toes.

"Don't you have another

daughter?" asked the prince, when Cinderella's stepmother finally admitted defeat.

"There is only Cinderella," she said, "and she's little more than a maid."

But the prince insisted that Cinderella try on the slipper and, of course, it fitted her perfectly. The prince peered at the shabby figure before him and smiled. Even through the dirt and grime, he could recognise the beautiful maiden he had danced with.

"My one true love," he cried, before lifting her onto his horse and riding away.

The Three Billy Goats Gruff

Once, high in some faraway mountains, lived three Billy Goats Gruff. There was a teeny, tiny billy goat, a middle-sized billy goat and a big, strong billy goat.

One day, when the teeny, tiny Billy Goat Gruff was searching for some juicy grass to eat, he noticed a meadow full of green, green grass on the other side of the river. "Hmm," he thought, "if I could just cross over that bridge and eat some of that grass I could grow as big as my brothers."

But every smart Billy Goat Gruff knew that an ugly troll lived under the bridge. A troll who was so bad and ugly that any goat who dared to set foot on the bridge was never heard of again.

"I've never seen him," thought the teeny, tiny Billy Goat Gruff. "Perhaps he's moved away. That grass looks so very delicious, I think I'll just tiptoe across and hope for the best!"

So the brave little Billy Goat Gruff tiptoed his way across the bridge.

TRIP, TRAP! TRIP, TRAP! TRIP, TRAP!

went his hooves. He was halfway across the bridge when suddenly, "ROAR", out jumped the horrible troll. "Who's that trip, trapping over my bridge?" roared the troll.

"Only little old me," said the teeny, tiny Billy Goat Gruff. "I'm on my way to the meadow to eat grass. Don't let me disturb you."

"Oh, no, you don't," roared the ugly troll.

"You've woken me up and now I'm going to gobble you up."

"But I'm just a skinny thing," said the teeny, tiny Billy Goat Gruff. "Hardly a snack really. Why don't you wait for my middle-sized brother to come along? There's far more meat on him."

"Okay, okay," roared the nasty troll. "Now hurry along before I change my mind."

Later, when the middle-sized Billy Goat Gruff saw his teeny, tiny brother enjoying the green, green grass on the other side of the bridge, he decided to join him.

TRIP, TRAP!
TRIP, TRAP!
TRIP, TRAP!

went his hooves as he tiptoed over the bridge.

But he was only halfway across, when,

114

"ROAR", out jumped the evil troll. "Who's that trip, trapping over my bridge?" he roared.

"Only me," said the middle-sized Billy Goat Gruff. "I'm off to the far meadow to eat green grass. I hope I didn't wake you."

"Oh, no, you don't," roared the nasty troll. "You've disturbed me while I'm fishing, and now I'm going to gobble you up."

"But I'm not very big," said the middle-sized Billy Goat Gruff. "I'm all coat really. Why don't you wait for my big brother to come along? He's big and fat. He would make you a proper feast."

"All right," roared the troll. "But hurry up before I change my mind."

The big Billy Goat Gruff could hardly believe his eyes when he saw his brothers enjoying the green, green grass on the other side of the bridge. "They will finish it all if I'm not quick," he thought, as he tiptoed his way across the bridge. But he had barely gone more than a few paces before,

"ROAR", out leapt the horrible troll.

"Who's that trip, trapping over my bridge?" roared the troll.

"Just me," said the big Billy Goat Gruff. "I'm on my way to the meadow to eat grass."

"Oh, no, you're not!" roared the troll. "I've heard all about you and now I'm going to gobble you up."

"Oh, no, you're not," roared the biggest Billy Goat Gruff. Then he lowered his horns and charged!

"Ahhhh!" screamed the nasty troll, as the biggest

Billy Goat Gruff tossed him into the air. "Heeelp!" he screamed, as he flew higher and higher, until, SPLASH, he fell into the deepest part of the river.

Without looking back, the biggest Billy Goat Gruff raced to join his brothers. And from that day onwards the three Billy Goats Gruff and all their friends could cross over the bridge to eat the green, green grass whenever they wanted. As for the troll, well, no one ever heard of him again.

The Little Fir Tree

Deep in the forest grew a little fir tree. He was a very pretty fir tree, but he was not happy. He hated being so small and wished he was as tall as the trees who towered above him.

"Oh, if only I was tall, like you," he said to an oak. "Then I'd be able to look out over the world, and birds would nest in my branches."

"Your time will come," said a friendly stork. "Why don't you enjoy being young? Just look how the sun warms you,

118

and the birds and animals play around you."

But the little fir tree refused to listen. Instead, he dreamed of things yet to come. One day woodcutters came and cut down the tallest trees.

"Where are they going?" the little fir tree asked.

"Ah," squawked the stork. "I've seen trees like that sailing the seven seas, because they have been made into the masts of ships."

Well, the little fir tree thought being a mast and sailing the seven seas sounded much better than hanging out in a boring old forest. After that, he spent so much time dreaming of a life at sea that he barely noticed when summer turned to fall, then fall to winter.

Christmas drew near and men came to dig up the tallest fir trees and take them away.

"Where are they taking them?" the little fir tree asked the stork.

"Ah," squawked the stork. "They are taken into people's houses and decorated with balls and ribbons."

The little tree trembled with excitement. "Oh, that sounds even better than sailing the seven seas. That's what I want to do."

Another year passed, and the little fir tree grew taller and stronger. Christmas came once more, and men came to dig up trees.

"Pick me! Pick me!" cried the little fir tree. Of course, the men couldn't hear him, but because the little fir tree was so handsome he was the first to be dug up.

"Bye-bye," he shouted to his friends, as he was carted away.

Despite the bumpy road, the little fir tree enjoyed his ride into town. However, he was pleased when the cart pulled up outside a fine house and he was lifted off the cart. A man, a woman and two children came out of the house.

"Isn't it handsome," cried the woman.

"Isn't it tall," cried the man.

120

"Isn't it pretty," cried the children.

The little fir tree trembled with pride as he was taken into the house and stood in a wooden bucket.

"So this is my new home," he thought. "It's so much grander than the forest. And my new friends say the nicest things."

The little fir tree thought he would burst with happiness when the children came and decorated him. And when the man placed a gold star on his highest tip, he felt like the smartest little fir tree that had ever lived.

The next day was even better. First, the children sat around him to open their presents. Then there was singing and dancing. Oh, how the little fir tree wished he could join in.

In the evening, the children sat around the little fir tree while their father told them wonderful stories. The little fir tree had never heard such tales. It really was the best day of his life.

Long after everyone had gone to bed, the fir tree shook with glee. He couldn't believe what an important little tree he was, nor could he wait to see what happened tomorrow.

Early next morning, the little fir tree stood ready for action. He waited and waited, but nobody came. Then he heard footsteps and voices.

"We'd better get that tree out of here before it starts dropping needles," said the woman.

"Come on, children. Let's take it out," said the man. They picked up the fir tree and carried it from the room.

"Let's put it in the shed," said the man.

It was very quiet and very dark in the shed. The little fir tree didn't like it one bit. He was left there for days and days, and had nothing to do but think.

"I miss the forest," thought the fir tree. "I had so

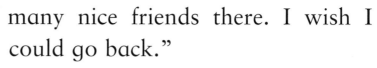

many nice friends there. I wish I could go back."

One day, the shed door swung open. The children had come in search of their sledges. "Hey, it's the Christmas tree," cried the little girl.

"Let's take it into the garden and plant it," said the little boy.

"What now?" thought the fir tree, as he was dragged from the shed and planted in the ground.

At first it felt cold to be outside once more, but as the sun warmed his trunk and birds rested in his branches, the fir tree began to glow with happiness.

A large bird landed beside the fir tree. "So this is where you got to. I've missed you." It was the stork.

The little fir tree trembled with excitement. This was the life – outside, where a fir tree really belonged!

The Pied Piper of Hamelin

Hamelin was a lovely little town, full of narrow, cobbled streets and wood-framed houses. The people who lived there had a very good life. However, they weren't at all happy. They weren't happy because their town was overrun with rats.

Thousands and thousands of rats swarmed the streets and ran through the houses. They raided pantries, ransacked rubbish, ate through doorways and walls, frightened children – and even attacked the town's cats. They were everywhere – even in beds and baths! Something had to be done.

After the townspeople had tried everything, from poisons and potions to rat traps and rat cats, they began to despair. One afternoon, they gathered together and marched to the mayor's house.

"Enough is enough," cried the crowd. "The rats are eating our food and making our children fall ill. The rats must go, or we will make sure that you do."

"Good people," smiled the mayor. "I will not rest until our town is rid of this deadly plague of rats. This very afternoon I will send out a proclamation offering 100 gold coins to anyone who can rid this town of rats. It will be a small price for us to pay."

And so the mayor issued his proclamation. In the following days, all kinds of people arrived in Hamelin to try their hand at getting rid of the rats. There were magicians and merchants, soldiers and scientists. But one after another, each one gave up and returned home.

125

Then, just as the mayor was about to give up hope, a stranger knocked on the door of the town hall. A very odd-looking fellow, wearing a colourful patched cloak and a pointed hat, stood in front of the mayor. In his hand, the stranger carried a long musical pipe.

"What is your business?" asked the mayor, frowning at the man and his pipe. "This isn't a good time. The town is far too busy with rats to be bothered with music."

"Aha! Well, I'm your man," laughed the stranger. "I can get rid of all your rats before nightfall."

The mayor secretly thought that the stranger looked a bit odd, but out loud he said, "You certainly look like the man for the job.

As soon as the rats are gone I will hand over 100 gold coins. By the way, what is your name?"

"I am the Pied Piper," said the stranger. Then he was gone.

The Pied Piper walked to the main street. He placed his pipe to his lips and began to play a haunting melody. Before he had played more than a handful of notes, there was a rumbling sound and a huge swarm of rats appeared. Rat after rat streamed after the mysterious piper as he walked through the narrow streets, playing his magical tune.

The rats poured out of houses, holes, gutters, barns, workshops and ditches. They followed the stranger on and on, until he came to a fast-running stream. Then, as the piper stood at the water's

edge, all the rats plunged into the water and drowned.

The people of Hamelin were overjoyed. Church bells rang out all over the town, and the townspeople quickly arranged a street party to celebrate.

As the whole town danced around in celebration, the Pied Piper appeared before the mayor.

"What now?" said the mayor, frowning at the odd-looking fellow.

"My 100 gold coins, if you please?" said the Pied Piper, holding out his hand.

But the mayor just laughed. "You want 100 gold coins for tricking a few silly rats with a pipe. Anyone could do that. Besides, the rats have drowned. There's no way you can bring them back. I tell you what, I'll give you 50 gold coins. Isn't that generous?"

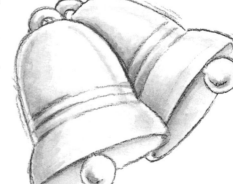

"Quite, quite," shouted the townspeople, who soon seemed to have forgotten the misery that the rats had brought. "Fifty gold coins is more than he deserves. Why, he's little more than a beggar!"

"I have kept my side of the bargain," said the Pied Piper. "Now I want payment in full. If you won't hand it over, I will be forced to play a tune that this whole town will live to regret."

"Carry on like this, and you'll not get a penny," cried the mayor. And the townspeople all quickly agreed that the stranger should get nothing at all.

Without saying another word, the Pied Piper walked to the outskirts of town, where he placed his pipe to his lips and began to play his haunting melody. The adults stood spellbound, as the town's children stopped what they were doing and skipped after the piper. Laughing, the boys and girls scrambled down steps and up hills, just as the rats had done.

The mayor and the townspeople looked on helplessly as the Pied Piper headed for the stream where the rats had drowned. They let out a sigh of relief when he used the bridge to cross to the other side, then headed uphill towards a large mountain. All this time the children were following him.

"There's no way they can get over that mountain," said the mayor. "He'll have to bring them back."

However, the mayor was wrong. When the Pied Piper got to the mountain, he played a few special notes and an opening appeared in the hillside. The Piper slipped through and the children followed him. Then the opening closed, and the only thing that could be

heard was a distant sobbing. It was the tears of a small boy who had been left behind because he was too slow.

Later, the small boy told the townspeople how the Pied Piper had promised to take the children to a wonderful kingdom of laughter and games, where they could all live happily for ever. The mayor and his people didn't know whether to believe the story, but they never saw the children again.

From that day on, the sound of children's laughter was never heard in the sad streets of Hamelin again. How the people wished that they had kept their promise to the Piper.

The Twelve Dancing Princesses

Once upon a time there was a king who had twelve beautiful daughters. During the day, the girls were model princesses. But at night, the king didn't know what they got up to. It was very puzzling, because although he carefully locked the door to their room, by morning all their shoes were worn out as if they had been out dancing all night long.

Buying new shoes for his twelve princess daughters was costing the king a lot of money, and he was getting annoyed.

The king

announced that whoever discovered where the twelve princesses danced at night could choose his favourite for his bride.

Before long, twelve noble princes took up the challenge. Each one sat guard, in a chair, beside a princess's bed. But before the clock struck twelve, the princes were all asleep. When they awoke in the morning, the princesses had clearly been dancing, because their shoes were full of holes. And so the twelve princes left the kingdom empty-handed.

One day, a poor soldier was passing through the forest near the castle, when he met an old woman who lived there. "Where are you going?" she asked the soldier.

"I thought I'd go and find out where the princesses dance each night," he explained.

"I see," cackled the old woman. "Well, that

shouldn't be too hard. But make sure you don't drink anything those princesses offer you." Then she gave him a cloak. "As soon as you put this on you will be invisible," she explained. "That way, you will be able to follow the princesses without their knowing it."

So the poor soldier went to the castle to try his luck. That night, as he prepared to sit guard, the eldest princess brought him a glass of water. Remembering the old woman's warning, the soldier threw the water away. Then he sat back and pretended to snore.

When the princesses heard his snores, they started to dress. After they'd pulled on the new shoes that the king had bought that very day, they checked that the soldier was still sleeping. Satisfied that the sleeping potion she had given him had worked, the eldest princess went to her bed and clapped her hands.

The soldier, who was peeking through half-closed eyes, was amazed to see the bed sink into the floor, and a trapdoor swing open. He watched quietly as each of the princesses went through the trapdoor one by one.

When the last princess had disappeared, the soldier leaped to his feet, threw the cloak around his shoulders, and became invisible.

Thinking that there wasn't a moment to lose, he raced down the stairs so fast that he stepped on the youngest princess's dress.

"Someone has hold of my gown," cried the princess. But the other princesses told her not to be silly and hurried her along.

At the bottom of the stairs, the soldier followed the princesses through a door into beautiful woodland. The silver leaves on the trees sparkled so brilliantly that the soldier decided to break one off and take it home.

"What was that?" asked the youngest princess. "I'm sure someone is following us."

The other princesses told her not to be silly and hurried her along.

At the edge of the wood, they came to a lake. At the side of the lake lay twelve boats, with twelve handsome princes waiting beside them. By

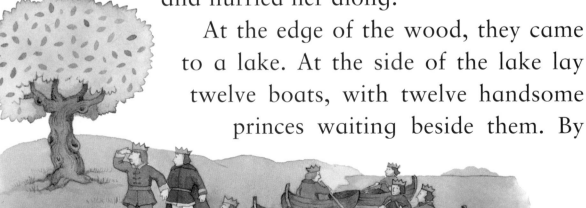

the time a princess and a prince had gotten into each of the boats, they looked so overloaded that the soldier thought they would sink if he got in too.

He eyed each of the princesses in turn. "Who is the lightest?" he wondered. Finally, he decided that the youngest princess was the lightest by far. But even so, the boat rocked and creaked as he got into it.

Halfway across the lake, the prince rowing the boat with the youngest princess and the invisible soldier complained that it felt heavier than usual. "Have you put on weight?" he asked the princess.

"Don't be silly," said the youngest princess, and she hurried him on his way.

On the other side of the lake was a golden castle. The soldier followed the twelve princes and twelve princesses into the castle, and watched them dance the whole night through.

Then, just before dawn, still covered by his invisible cloak, he followed the princesses home.

When they reached the stairs

leading to their bedroom, the soldier overtook them, threw off his cloak, and lay snoring in the chair before any of the princesses had climbed into the room through the trapdoor.

Seeing the soldier still fast asleep, the princesses thought their secret was safe.

The following morning, the soldier showed the king the silver leaf he had broken from a branch, and explained what he had seen.

The king was very happy, and asked which of the princesses he would choose for his bride.

The soldier chose the youngest, whom he thought prettier and smarter than any of her sisters. She was delighted, for she thought the soldier even handsomer than her prince.

Shortly after this, the soldier and the princess were married. Afterwards, there was a wonderful ball. The youngest princess danced with her new husband until midnight. And as for her eleven sisters? Well, they danced until dawn!

The Tin Soldier

Long ago, in a faraway toy room, there were twenty-five tin soldiers. They all stood at attention in their smart blue-and-white uniforms, and each of them proudly carried a musket (which, as any old soldier will tell you, is an old-fashioned sort of gun) in their arms.

They were all exactly the same, except for one, who only had one leg. You see, he had been the very last to be made, and when they got around to him they had run short of tin; so he only had one leg because there wasn't enough tin for two.

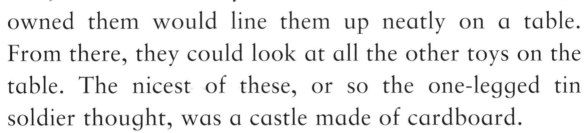

The one-legged tin soldier stood just as firmly on his one leg as his brothers did on two. In fact, some might say even firmer.

When the tin soldiers weren't sleeping in their box, the little boy who owned them would line them up neatly on a table. From there, they could look at all the other toys on the table. The nicest of these, or so the one-legged tin soldier thought, was a castle made of cardboard.

The one-legged tin soldier spent hours gazing at that castle. He knew every little tree and creature that surrounded it. He thought they were lovely, but the loveliest of them all was a tiny lady who stood in a doorway. Though the tin soldier didn't know it, the lady was a dancer. She was dressed in a beautiful lace dress and wore a red rose, made from a tiny piece of tin, in her hair. She stretched out both arms, and held one leg so high in the air, the way dancers can, so that the one-legged tin soldier

couldn't see it. Because of this, he thought she only had one leg, just like him.

"She'd make me a perfect wife," thought the tin soldier. "But she's much too grand. After all, she lives in a splendid castle, while I only have a box to call home. And I have to share that with my twenty-four brothers. But I'd like to speak to her, anyway."

So the one-legged tin soldier hid behind a Jack-in-the-box that stood on the table, and kept quiet.

Later that night, when all the other tin soldiers had been put away, and the people of the house had gone to bed, the toys blinked their eyes, stretched their arms and legs, and began to play.

The other tin soldiers rattled in their box and shouted angrily because they couldn't open the locked lid. The clockwork mouse raced across the table,

the spinning top spun and the toy train whizzed around and around on its track.

The only toys that didn't move were the dancer and the one-legged tin soldier. The dancer just stood there with her arms high in the air, and the tin soldier just stood at attention as he stared at her.

At midnight the clock struck twelve, and the lid of the Jack-in-the-box, behind which the tin soldier was hiding, flew open. All the toys knew that the Jack-in-the-box was something of an evil magician.

"Don't you know that staring is rude," the Jack-in-the-box shouted at the tin soldier. But the tin soldier was not scared, and paid no attention. He clung to his musket and stood at attention.

"You just wait until tomorrow," said the Jack-in-the-box, before springing back into his box.

The next morning, when the maid was cleaning the toy room, the one-legged tin soldier was put on the windowsill out of the way. And there he stood at attention, until a gust of wind blew him out the window. It could have been an accident, but the tin soldier couldn't help thinking that the Jack-in-the-box had worked some sort of magic.

It was a long way to the pavement below and the tin soldier landed with quite a bump. But, being a brave soldier, he didn't make a sound. He just clung to his musket and stood at attention, even though it had started to rain.

It rained so hard that the drains of the streets began

to fill with water. Eventually, though, it stopped raining and some children came out to play.

"Wow, look! A tin soldier," said a little girl. "Let's make him a boat and send him sailing down the drain."

So the tin soldier found himself afloat in a boat made of newspaper. The boat rocked and swayed as it made its way along the drain but the tin soldier never stopped standing at attention, even when the boat whirled down a dark sewer pipe.

"What's going to happen to me now?" thought the soldier. "It's all that Jack-in-the-box's fault. If only I had that one-legged lady with me, I wouldn't be so afraid of the dark."

At that moment, the tin soldier

heard a rustle and a scratch, and a big, ugly water rat jumped out of a hole in the side of the sewer. "Passport please!" shouted the water rat.

But the tin soldier said nothing and sailed on. The water rat followed him. "Stop that soldier!" he cried. "He has not shown his passport. I don't even think he has one!" But no one paid any attention and the water rat was unable to keep up with the paper boat.

The tin soldier was swept on and on. Soon he could see daylight at the end of the tunnel. Then he heard a roaring sound and before he could blink he was swept into a powerful waterfall. The boat spun round and round as it was washed into a canal below. But the tin soldier never cried out, for soldiers did not do such things.

The tin soldier stood at attention as the paper boat began to sink. Soon he was up to his neck in water, but he still stood at attention. Then the boat split in two and the tin soldier sank down through the water. The tin soldier felt sure that he was going to drown and wished that the little dancer was with him.

Then, all of a sudden, GULP, the tin soldier was swallowed by a large fish. It was even darker inside the fish than it had been in the sewer. And it was narrower, too. Once more, the tin soldier wished that the dancer were by his side.

The fish swam up and down for what seemed like ages. Then, suddenly, it began wriggling this way and that. Then, just as suddenly, it became very still. The tin soldier stood

GULP!

at attention and wondered what was happening in this dark, dark place. He heard a strange swishing sound, and the next moment it wasn't dark anymore; daylight was shining down on him.

"Hey, it's the tin soldier," cried a familiar voice. It was the maid who had put him on the windowsill earlier that morning. You see, the fish had been caught in the canal and taken to market, where the maid had bought him and carried him home. Now that the fish had been cut open by a large kitchen knife, the tin soldier was free once more.

After he'd been washed, the tin soldier was taken back to the toy room and stood beside his toy soldier brothers on the table.

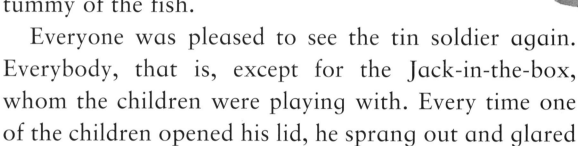

Everything was just as it had been before he left. How the children laughed and marvelled when they heard how the one-legged tin soldier had arrived back home in the tummy of the fish.

Everyone was pleased to see the tin soldier again. Everybody, that is, except for the Jack-in-the-box, whom the children were playing with. Every time one of the children opened his lid, he sprang out and glared at the tin soldier, as if to say, "Just you wait."

But the tin soldier was not scared of the Jack-in-the-box's magic.

He stood at attention and felt his heart lift as he saw that the dancer

was standing in exactly the same place as before. He looked at her and she looked at him, but neither of them said a word.

Suddenly, a gust of wind came through the window and blew the one-legged tin soldier from the table into the fire. "It's sure to be the Jack-in-the-box's doing," thought the tin soldier, as the flames melted his blue-and-white uniform. Then he started to bend as the fire melted his body.

A door opened, and the breeze caught hold of the tiny paper dancer and blew her straight into the fire too. The one-

148

legged tin soldier and the dancer stared at each other for one last time as they both disappeared in the flames.

When the maid cleaned out the fire the next morning, she was surprised to find something nestling among the ashes. The tin soldier had melted into the shape of a little tin heart, and the red tin rose, from the hair of the little dancer, was stuck firmly to it. The maid carefully placed the little heart with the red rose on the mantlepiece, where it stayed for many years to come. The one-legged tin soldier and the dancer were together at last!

Snow White

Once there were a king and queen who lived in a distant land. They were very happy, except for one thing – they had no children.

"Oh," said the queen, "how I wish I had a daughter with skin as white as snow, hair as black as a raven's wing, and lips as red as cherries."

Within a year the queen's wish was granted and they had a beautiful baby girl, whom they called Snow White. Soon after her birth, the poor queen died and the king eventually remarried.

The new queen was very beautiful, but also very vain and very wicked. She could not bear to think that anyone was more beautiful than her. Every day she would stand in front of a magic mirror, and say:

*"Mirror, mirror,
on the wall,
Who is the fairest
of them all?"*
And the mirror would reply:
*"You are the fairest
one of all."*

However, as the years passed, Snow White grew up to become more and more beautiful, until one day the magic mirror told the wicked queen: *"You were the fairest, shining bright, But now much fairer is Snow White."*

The queen was furious. She sent for a servant. She told the servant to take Snow White into the forest and

leave her there for the wild animals to eat. And so it was that Snow White found herself alone in the forest. At first she was scared, but soon the animals took pity on her and led her to a pretty little cottage. She knocked on the door and, when there was no answer, she walked right in. The inside of the cottage was as pretty as the outside. In the middle of the room stood a neat little table, set with seven places and surrounded by seven little chairs.

Feeling hungry and thirsty, Snow White took a little bread from each of the plates and a little milk from each of the cups. Then, feeling tired, she curled up on one of the seven beds and fell into a deep sleep.

The cottage belonged to seven dwarfs. Every

morning they left their cottage to dig for jewels and gold in the hills. And every evening they returned home to eat and sleep.

When they returned home that night, they noticed at once that they had a visitor.

"Somebody has been eating my bread," said one.

"Somebody has been drinking my milk," said another.

"Somebody has been sleeping in my bed," said another. "Look, she's still here!"

Quickly, all the dwarfs gathered around the bed to look at their sleeping visitor.

"Isn't she lovely?" said one.

"Let's leave her to sleep," said another. And so they left her until morning.

When Snow White awoke, the seven little dwarfs were gathered around her bed.

153

They were so kind that she told them her story.

The dwarfs all agreed that Snow White should stay with them. Each day, when they went to dig for jewels and gold in the hills, Snow White stayed home, cleaning and cooking.

And so the years passed, and Snow White grew more and more beautiful.

Meanwhile the queen, thinking that Snow White was dead, hadn't bothered looking in her mirror. Then one day, she thought she felt a spot growing on her chin and went to the mirror to check. While she was there, she asked:

"*Mirror, mirror, on the wall,*

Who is the fairest of them all?"

You can just imagine her surprise when it replied:

"*In the dwarfs' house, in yonder hill, Snow White is the fairest still.*"

The queen turned red with fury. Determined to get rid of Snow White once and for all, she quickly began to plot and plan. The following morning the queen dressed up as an old

154

woman. Then she filled a basket with pretty things and went to the dwarfs' cottage.

"Buy something from a poor old woman," she cackled. Of course, Snow White, being such a kind-hearted young girl, let her in at once.

"Oh, these are ever so pretty," said Snow White, pulling some ribbons from the basket.

"Yes, just perfect for lacing your dress," agreed the old woman. Snow White let the old woman lace her dress with a colourful ribbon.

But the wicked queen pulled the ribbon so tight that Snow White fell to the ground. The wicked queen thought that she was dead.

When the seven dwarfs arrived home, they rushed to Snow White's side and quickly untied the ribbon. Snow White gulped a huge breath and soon recovered.

"It must have been the wicked queen," decided the dwarfs.

"From now on you must always be watchful. When we're away from home, you mustn't let anyone in."

Meanwhile, the queen had raced back to the castle and rushed to the mirror:

"Mirror, mirror, on the wall,
Who is the fairest of them all?"

And the mirror replied:

"In the dwarfs' house, in yonder hill,
Snow White is the fairest still."

The queen couldn't believe her ears. Once again, she began to plot and plan.

In the morning, the queen called at the dwarfs' house, dressed as a beggar woman with a basket of pretty combs – combs she had dipped in poison!

"I can't let you in," Snow White shouted from the window.

"Never mind," croaked the old woman. "Why don't you just try this pretty comb in your lovely hair?"

The comb was so pretty that Snow White leaned out of the window and allowed the old woman to push it into her hair. As soon as the comb touched Snow White's skin, she fell to the ground.

Luckily for Snow White, the seven dwarfs came home early that day. When they saw her lying there, they guessed what had happened and removed the comb from her hair at once. Again, Snow White was quick to recover. Once again, the dwarfs warned her about strangers.

The queen, meanwhile, was in a rage for she had just been told:

"In the dwarfs' house, in yonder hill,
Snow White is the fairest still."

Now she was more determined than ever to destroy Snow White. So the next morning, she picked an apple that was half red and half green, and injected poison into one half of it. Then, dressed as a farmer's wife, she called on Snow White.

"I just want to give you this juicy apple," smiled the farmer's wife, holding up the half-red and half-green

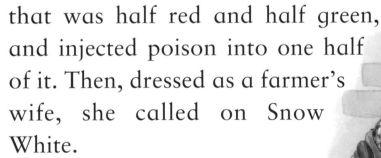

apple. "Look, it's not poisoned. I'll take a bite from it myself." And she took a bite from the half of the apple that wasn't poisoned.

Seeing that the apple did the farmer's wife no harm, Snow White accepted it and took a bite. But as soon as she did, she fell down as if dead.

That night, when the dwarfs arrived home, there was nothing they could do to wake Snow White for, although she was not dead, she was in a very deep sleep – a sleep so deep that it seemed as though she would never wake.

Feeling very sad, the seven dwarfs built her a glass coffin and placed her in the hills, where all who passed could admire her beauty, for, although she slept for year after year, her beauty never changed. Her skin remained as white as snow, her hair was as black as a raven's wing, and her lips were as red as cherries.

Then one day, a handsome prince saw the glass coffin and fell in love with the sleeping princess.

"You must let me take her back to my castle," said

the prince. "I cannot live without seeing such beauty each day."

At first the dwarfs were reluctant to agree, but finally they saw that the prince loved Snow White, and they agreed to let him take her.

Very carefully, the seven dwarves lifted the glass coffin onto their shoulders and started down the hillside. But they stumbled, and the piece of poisoned apple was shaken from Snow White's throat.

She awoke at once. And, on seeing the prince, she too fell in love.

It was a grand wedding. The whole kingdom was invited, and all agreed that the bride was the fairest of them all.

Meanwhile, the wicked queen had discovered that her evil plan had failed. In her anger, she smashed her mirror and never looked at her reflection again.

Thumbelina

Once upon a time, there was a woman who wanted to have a child of her own. The years passed by and no child came. One day the woman went to see a witch. The witch gave her a stem of barley and told the woman to plant it in a flowerpot.

The woman did as she was told, and a beautiful flower grew. The petals of the flower were shut tight, so the woman kissed them. At once, the petals sprang open and the woman saw a tiny baby girl inside. The little girl was beautiful, but she was even tinier than the woman's thumb. The woman and her husband decided to call her Thumbelina.

They gave the baby a walnut shell for a bed and a rose leaf for a blanket. She slept in the bed at night and played on the table during the daytime.

Then, one night, an ugly toad jumped onto the table where Thumbelina slept.

"RIBBET!"

"RIBBET!" croaked the toad. "She would make a perfect wife for my son." The toad grabbed Thumbelina as she slept and carried her away to her muddy home.

"RIBBET! RIBBET!" croaked her ugly son,

161

when he saw the beautiful Thumbelina.

"EEEK," screamed Thumbelina, when she saw the two ugly toads. "Ahhh!" she wailed, when the mother toad explained that she wanted Thumbelina to marry her ugly son.

The toads were afraid that Thumbelina might run away. They took her to a lily pad on the river. There was no way that Thumbelina could escape. She cried and she cried. When they heard her sobs, the little fish poked their heads out of the water. Charmed by her beauty, they decided to help the tiny girl. They chewed away at the stem that held the lily pad in place, until at last it was free. Thumbelina floated away.

She floated on and on down the river. Then, one day,

the wind blew so hard that Thumbelina was swept up into the air and carried onto the land.

All through the summer, Thumbelina lived alone in a big wood. However, when the winter came she soon felt hungry. She left the wood and made her way into a field. Before too long, she came to a door and knocked on it. When it was opened by a field mouse, Thumbelina begged her for something to eat. Luckily, the field mouse was a kind creature and she invited Thumbelina into her warm home. The field mouse soon grew to like Thumbelina and invited her to stay.

After Thumbelina had been there for a short time, the field mouse told her about her neighbour, Mr Mole.

"He's a very rich man. It would be wonderful if you could marry him. Of course, he is blind, so you will have to please him with your pretty voice."

But after meeting Mr Mole, Thumbelina did not

want to marry him at all. He was indeed rich, but he hated the sunlight and the flowers although he had never seen them. Mr Mole fell in love as soon as he heard Thumbelina's sweet voice. The field mouse and Mr Mole agreed that he would marry Thumbelina.

Mr Mole dug a tunnel between their two houses, and one day he gave Thumbelina a guided tour.

Halfway along the tunnel, Mr Mole kicked aside a dead bird.

"Stupid thing," he grumbled. "It must have died at the beginning of the winter." Thumbelina felt sorry for the bird, but she said nothing.

Later, when the field mouse was asleep, Thumbelina

crept back into the tunnel. "Good-bye, dear bird," she whispered. She pressed her head against the bird's chest and, to her surprise, she felt something move. The bird was not dead. It had lain asleep all winter and was now waking up.

For the rest of the winter, Thumbelina nursed the bird and soon he was well. When spring arrived, Thumbelina smuggled him in through the tunnel and out of the field mouse's door.

"Good-bye," wept Thumbelina, as the bird flew away.

Time passed quickly, and soon Thumbelina's wedding day arrived. Wishing to get one last look at the outside world before entering Mr Mole's gloomy home, she walked in the field.

"*Quiveet, quiveet,*" came a noise above her head. It was Thumbelina's bird friend. Seeing how unhappy the little girl was, he said, "I'm flying somewhere warm for the winter. Come with me. You can sit on my back."

Thumbelina quickly agreed and before too long she found herself in a wonderful warm place. The bird put Thumbelina down on the petals of a beautiful flower. To Thumbelina's surprise, a tiny man with wings was sitting in the centre of the flower. He was a flower fairy. Straight away he fell in love with the tiny Thumbelina and asked her to marry him. Thumbelina happily agreed.

On their wedding day, Thumbelina received all kinds of presents. The best one of all was a pair of tiny wings. She used them to fly from flower to flower. At last Thumbelina was the happiest girl alive!

Beauty and the Beast

Once upon a time there was a rich merchant who lived in a grand house with his three beautiful daughters. The girls were given everything they wanted and were waited on by an army of servants.

The two eldest sisters were very vain and very spoilt but the youngest, who was also the prettiest, was kind and sweet. Indeed, she was so pretty and kind that everyone called her 'Beauty'.

All three girls led a fine life and couldn't have been happier. Then one day, disaster struck. Their father lost his fortune and so they had to move to a tiny cottage in the woods. The two eldest girls were not at all happy and spent every day grumbling and squabbling. But Beauty couldn't have been happier. She loved the little cottage and enjoyed cleaning it and tending its little garden.

And so they settled into their new life, until one day their father was called away on business. It was a trip that promised to help give them back their fortune, so you can imagine how everyone was excited. Before he left, the merchant asked each of his daughters what present she would like him to bring back. The two elder girls reeled off an endless list.

"Pearl necklace... diamond brooch... velvet gown... silk scarves... gold ring..." said one.

"Emerald bracelet... sapphire earrings... silk gown... silver comb... gold slippers..." said the other.

However, when the merchant asked Beauty what she would like, she thought for a moment, then said, "What I would wish for most of all is a single red rose. We have none in our garden, and I do love them so."

This simple request brought

169

a tear to the merchant's eye that stayed with him throughout his long journey.

The trip proved a success and the merchant travelled home a much richer man. He had bought the dresses and jewels the elder daughters had asked for, and was searching for a red rose for Beauty when he became quite lost.

As night began to fall, the weary traveller looked around for shelter, and was surprised to come across a grand palace hidden deep in the woods. On the palace gates was a bold sign, which read:

WELCOME
ALL
TRAVELLERS

As the merchant approached the gates, they swung open as if inviting him in. The merchant looked around, but no one was there. He shrugged his shoulders in surprise, then hurried to put his horse in the well-kept, but empty, stable. After he had fed and watered the horse, he knocked on the palace door. No one answered, but the palace door swung open.

The merchant wandered through the palace. All the rooms were richly furnished and fires burned in all the grates, but no one was there. In one of the rooms, a tempting meal was laid out on a table. The merchant waited to see if anyone would come, but eventually hunger got the better of him and he sat down to dine alone.

When he had finished eating, the merchant looked around for a place to sleep. In one of the bedrooms, the bed was made and, remembering the sign on the gate, the merchant spent the night there.

The next morning, he awoke to find his clothes washed and neatly folded. And when he went downstairs, a fine breakfast was waiting.

After breakfast, the merchant decided to take a walk in the garden before leaving. It was a beautiful morning, and the flowers in the garden were beyond compare. As he walked beneath a climbing rose, the merchant remembered Beauty's request and reached up to pluck a single red rose.

As soon as he held the rose in his hand, he heard a terrible roar. Terrified, he turned to find an ugly beast racing towards him.

"How dare you steal my prize rose," snarled the Beast. "Is that how you repay me for letting you stay in my home?"

"But I was just picking the rose for my youngest daughter," began the merchant.

"I don't care," said the Beast. "You will pay heavily for your crime. You will become my prisoner, and never leave this place."

Thinking of his poor daughters, who would surely starve without him, the merchant begged to be let go. Eventually, the Beast agreed on the condition that one of the merchant's daughters came to live in the palace.

The merchant returned home with a heavy heart. Upon hearing his story, Beauty insisted that she went to live with the Beast. Reluctantly, and after much argument, the merchant finally agreed.

When the merchant took Beauty to the palace, it was just as empty as on his first visit. But after they had eaten a meal, the Beast appeared. Beauty had never seen anything so ugly, but she tried to hide her fear.

"So you have come in your father's place," said the Beast, as gently as he could. "You must love him very much."

"Yes," nodded Beauty, trying not to shrink away.

"You are a kind girl," said the Beast. "I will treat you well."

Seeing that the Beast

was so gentle with Beauty, the merchant felt less worried as he returned home.

And so Beauty's new life began. She spent each day alone in the palace, then in the evening was joined by the Beast. In time, Beauty grew fond of the Beast and began looking forward to his company.

At the end of each evening, just before leaving, the Beast would say, "Will you marry me, Beauty?"

And Beauty would always reply, politely, "No thank you, Beast."

Then the Beast would give a heavy sigh, and leave. But the next evening he would ask her again. And again Beauty would reply, "No thank you, Beast."

It made Beauty sad to think that she made the Beast unhappy, but there was no way she could marry such an ugly creature.

Beauty hadn't been living

in the palace for very long when she began to feel homesick. When the Beast, who was really quite kind and cared greatly for Beauty, realised what was wrong, he gave her an enchanted mirror.

Whenever Beauty looked into the mirror, she could see her family. In this way, she always knew what was happening in her father's house.

Beauty looked into the mirror each day, and each day was pleased to see her family looking happy. They had moved back into their big house and her father's business was doing well. Her sisters, who were as vain as ever, both found husbands and left home. Beauty was pleased for them, but felt sad to think that she would never be a bride.

Then one day, Beauty was feeling particularly homesick. She looked into her mirror to cheer herself up but got a terrible shock. For there was her father, ill in bed, with both of her sisters weeping at his side.

175

When the Beast came that evening, he saw that something was wrong and asked Beauty what was troubling her. Beauty quickly explained and begged the Beast to let her visit her father.

After much thought, the Beast reluctantly agreed to let her go, but he made her promise she wouldn't stay away for long.

The next morning, when Beauty awoke, she found herself not in the Beast's palace but in her father's house. As soon as her father saw her, his heart lifted and from that day on he began to get better.

Some weeks had passed, and her father had been well for some time, when Beauty remembered her promise to the Beast. She looked into her magic mirror, and was alarmed to see the Beast alone and dying. Immediately, she arranged for her father to take her back to the Beast's palace.

On arriving, she found the Beast lying beneath his beloved climbing rose.

"Please don't die," cried Beauty. "I couldn't live without you."

"I thought you'd forgotten all

about me and would never come back," said the Beast. "Without you, I had nothing to live for."

"Forgive me," sobbed Beauty. "When I saw that you were ill, I realised that I love you. I will marry you, if you'll still have me."

And as soon as she whispered those words, the Beast changed into a handsome prince!

The prince quickly explained that an evil witch had cast a spell, turning him into a Beast – a spell that could only be broken when somebody loved him and promised to marry him.

Beauty was delighted with her handsome prince, and couldn't wait to tell her father of her good fortune. Not long after, Beauty and the prince were married. And in her hands, Beauty carried a bunch of red roses from the Beast's rosebush.

The Three Little Pigs

Early one morning
The sun came out,
And out set three pigs
Snorting their snouts.
SNORT!

Snort!

Snort!

The three little pigs – Oink, Grunt and Curly – walked up the hills and down the dales until their cheeks were quite pink.

TEE-HEE!

They walked to the woods
Where the path split in three,
And the three little pigs said:
"TEE-HEE!"

TEE-HEE!

The pigs set off in different directions. Oink went this way, Grunt went that way and Curly went . . . well . . .

Curly felt sad
As she trotted alone,
But then found some straw
For building her home.
HOME!

When her house was finished, Curly gathered some extra straw to make a table and chair for the inside. And, last of all, she plaited a little straw bed so that she would have a cosy night's sleep. But . . .

Along came a wolf
With a scary big frown,
Sharp teeth and a huff
And a blow your house down.
DOWN!

Poor Curly. Her straw house was no more. How she ran and ran, up the hills and down the dales, to escape from that horrid wolf.
Meanwhile,

Grunt snapped some sticks
From branches of wood
To make a new home
In the best way she could.
HOME!

When her house was finished, Grunt gathered some extra sticks to make a table and chair for the inside. And, last of all, she wove a little stick bed so that she would have a cosy night's sleep.
But . . .

Along came the wolf
With a scary big frown,
Sharp teeth and a huff
And a blow your house down.
DOWN!

Poor Grunt. Her stick house was no more. How she ran and ran, up the hills and down the dales, to escape from that horrid wolf.
Meanwhile,

Oink was struggling
With big heavy bricks,
But a brick house was stronger
Than a house made with sticks.
STICKS? POOH!

When her house was finished, Oink gathered some extra bricks to make a table and chair for the inside. And, last of all, she stacked some bricks for a little brick bed so that she would have a . . . well . . . probably extremely uncomfortable sleep that night.

Meanwhile . . . Curly and Grunt were still running, up hills and down dales, until their cheeks were quite pink. They were running to the place where their sister had built her house made of bricks.

Curly and Grunt ran,
Ran all the way,
Away from the wolf
To Oink's house to stay.
HOORAY! HOORAY!
HOORAY!
When, of course . . .

Along came the wolf
With a scary big frown,
Sharp teeth and a huff
And a blow your house down.
DOWN! NOT DOWN!

Inside the brick house, Oink, Grunt and Curly felt very safe.

Outside the brick house, the wolf's cheeks were growing redder and redder and hotter and hotter from all that huffing and puffing.

The brick house stayed up,
The wolf tumbled down,
Down a steep hill,
Still wearing his frown.
SNORT! SWEET! SNORT!

When the wolf was gone, Grunt wove some sticks in a clever way to make three little chairs. Oink made two more brick beds – one for each of her sisters.

And Curly used her straw-plaiting skills to make a lovely soft mattress to put on top of the brick beds. And the three little pigs had a very cosy night's sleep. Goodnight!

The Elves and the Shoemaker

There was once a shoemaker who lived with his wife. The shoemaker worked very hard, but he never made much money.

In time, he became poorer and poorer. Then one day all he had left was one piece of leather. Just enough leather to make one pair of shoes. So that night, before going to bed, the shoemaker cut out the leather and left

it on his workbench, ready to sew in the morning.

That night the shoemaker had a restless night's sleep as he worried about what they would do once the leather was gone. But when the shoemaker went to the bench in the morning, he couldn't believe his eyes. In place of the cut-out pieces of leather, there stood the finest pair of shoes he'd ever seen. Every stitch on them was so small and neat that they could hardly be seen.

"I've never seen such shoes," the shoemaker told his wife.

They couldn't imagine who might have sewn them. But they proudly displayed them in the window anyway.

Later that morning, a grand lady came into the shop and tried them on. "I've never worn anything so comfortable," she declared. And she paid the shoemaker twice his normal

price for them.

The shoemaker was delighted. Now he had money to buy food and enough leather to make two pairs of shoes.

That evening, he carefully cut out the two pairs of shoes. Then he left them on his workbench, ready to stitch in the morning.

The next morning, the shoemaker was delighted to see two pairs of shoes in place of the leather. Once again, they were beautifully stitched.

Later that day, a noble lord came into the shop to buy shoes. The shoemaker showed him the two pairs, and he was so impressed that he tried both on. They fitted perfectly, so he bought both pairs for a lot of money.

Now the shoemaker had enough money to buy leather for four pairs of shoes.

That evening, before going

to bed, he carefully cut out the four pairs of shoes and left them on the bench. Once again, he fully intended to stitch them in the morning.

However, when he awoke the next morning, he found four perfect pairs of shoes sitting on his workbench. Once again, he sold the shoes for a great deal of money.

And so it went on. Each night the shoemaker cut out shoes ready to stitch in the morning. And each morning, he found in their place shoes so perfectly made that he couldn't see a bad stitch on them.

Day after day, rich customers came to the shoemaker's shop to buy the perfectly made shoes. So, in time, the shoemaker and his wife became quite rich. But they never took their good fortune for granted.

One evening, just before Christmas,

the shoemaker said to his wife, "Why don't we stay up this evening to see who stitches our shoes?"

The shoemaker's wife quickly agreed, and that night they hid behind some clothes hanging in the corner of the room, and waited.

For a long time nothing happened. Then at midnight two tiny little men danced into the room. The two little men, whom the shoemaker recognised as elves, had bare feet and were dressed in rags.

The two elves did not see the shoemaker and his wife, but climbed up onto the bench, sat down, and began stitching. They worked so fast that the shoemaker could hardly believe his eyes. They did not stop until all the work was done. Then they danced off into the night.

The next morning the shoemaker and his wife agreed that they should repay the elves in some way. After all, they had made them rich.

So that very day, they

went out and bought the finest material and the softest leather they could find. And that evening, they got to work making new clothes for the elves.

Night after night they worked on the clothes. At last, on Christmas Eve, everything was ready. Instead of leaving shoes on the bench, the shoemaker and his wife laid out the perfectly made outfits. Then they hid and waited.

At midnight, the elves danced into the room and climbed up onto the bench. They were surprised to see tiny matching outfits instead of shoes for stitching. Delighted, they dressed themselves in their new clothes. Then, laughing and singing, they danced out into the night.

After that, the shoemaker and his wife never saw the elves again. But they did not mind. They had repaid the favour, and from then on luck was always with them. In time they became very rich, and lived a long and happy life together.